the Christmas Fox

Anik McGrory

Alfred A. Knopf · New York

"Come!" drummed the woodpecker.
"A baby is coming. There's work to
be done. There's news to spread."

But the little fox stayed to dance
with the snowflakes.

"Come!" lowed the cow. "A baby is coming. There's a place to make warm with sweet-smelling hay."

But the little fox stayed to splash
in the stream.

"Come!" bleated the lamb.
"There are gifts to get ready
with soft, cozy wool."

But the little fox rolled in
the cold, snappy snow.

"Come!" whistled the bluebird.
"There are songs to sing the
baby to sleep."

But the little fox stayed to pounce
in the snowdrifts.

Come, whispered the stars.
There is light to shine to
brighten the path.

But the little fox had no light to shine.
He had no song to sing. He had no soft
wool to collect, no warm home to share.

"Come," said the donkey.
"Just come. It is enough."

So the little fox came into
the warm, glowing stable.

And the little fox brought joy . . .
and the baby smiled.